Asma Khaled has been writing stories since she was 10 years old. She used to write in Arabic and English and published them in the school papers.

Then she graduated with her American diploma and entered university to study Spanish language. So now, she writes in Arabic, Spanish, and English.

What About My Love? is her first published book to the world—her first true experience that she wanted to share with the world—to spread love, self-confidence, and hope.

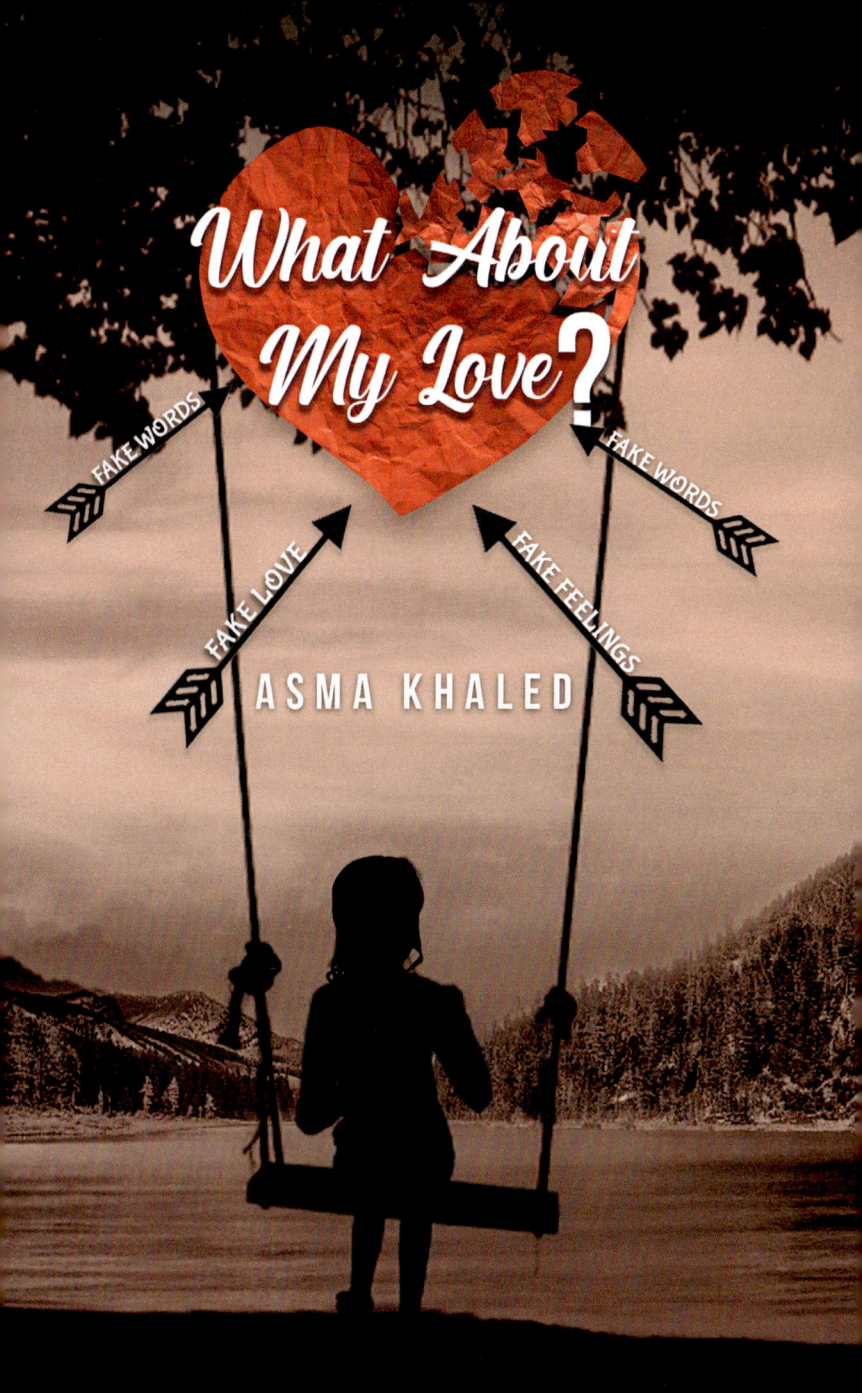

Copyright © Asma Khaled 2022

The right of **Asma Khaled** to be identified as author of this work has been asserted by the author in accordance with Federal Law No. (7) of UAE, Year 2002, Concerning Copyrights and Neighboring Rights.

All rights reserved. No part of this publication may be reproduced, stored in a retrieval system, or transmitted in any form or by any means, electronic, mechanical, photocopying, recording, or otherwise, without the prior permission of the publishers.

Any person who commits any unauthorized act in relation to this publication may be liable to legal prosecution and civil claims for damages.

ISBN – 9789948817772 – (Paperback)
ISBN – 9789948817765 – (E-Book)

Application Number: MC-10-01-7620295
Age Classification: E

The age group that matches the content of the books has been classified according to the age classification system issued by the National Media Council.

Printer Name: iPrint Global Ltd
Printer Address: Witchford, England

First Published 2022
AUSTIN MACAULEY PUBLISHERS FZE
Sharjah Publishing City
P.O. Box [519201]
Sharjah, UAE
www.austinmacauley.ae
+971 655 95 202

Dedicating this book to my mom, Amal, the hope of my life, who encouraged me to publish it and keep going.
My sister, Aisha Khaled, who taught me how to create the pictures that I want. She is so intelligent.
Finally, to myself, who had enough courage to write the story that changed my life and destroyed it, yet I decided to make it a successful experience and not a bad one.

Author's Note

I know all of us have been through a lot and many of us have chosen wrong, just like I did. And I know how painful it is to love hard and at the end, you end up realizing that you have chosen the wrong person. But you know what to do once you realize that, you leave and rise up again. It's never the end.

What About My Love?

Will I be able to give my love to another one? Shall I throw it away? Or shall I just forget it forever? Will I be able to even forget it?
As I tell you my story, you might think it seems common, yet it's different. Some people may not feel me but those who will definitely feel me have been through pain and failure as well. So how many of us haven't passed through hard times and pain, and to be specific: "love pain."

Chapter 1

In a very dark city near California, lived a very lovely, beautiful, full-of-life, and pure girl. I, Cassandra Daryl. I lived away from my parents due to some family conditions. But I was, in fact, enjoying life and happy with my friends; we were all in the same university. Despite the happiness I experienced, I felt alone sometimes, I felt that something was missing.

Mom and Dad called me every day to check up on me, we laughed together. I missed my parents every day but I couldn't let that control my life, so I studied hard to make my parents proud and to have the perfect future. But I, in fact, didn't plan for that upcoming event in my life.

It was a quiet night and I loved these types of nights, a very peaceful once. I sat on the couch relaxing a bit after finishing a dozen of assignments. Drinking my tea and holding my phone, finally. I found a friend request from an old friend, Erik Daemon, that I knew few months ago in college but we didn't really talk much. I was surprised to find his request but I accepted it at the end as I remembered my first interaction with him but it was not that important.

One day, I texted him to thank him because he helped my sister Alexa get back her stolen wallet and eye glasses. I was about to send her money when she told me that Erik had found it and given it back to her.
I was really happy so I decided to take his phone number to thank him myself.
"Hey, Erik, this is Cassandra, Alexa's sister. Just wanted to thank you for what you did for my sister," I texted.
"Hello, Cassandra. No need to thank me really, I didn't do anything and I am under your command anytime," Erik replied few hours later.
Wow! What a gentleman! I thought.

So after accepting him, we started talking every day, we started getting used to each other, and we got to know each other even more. I started feeling something different with time, I started getting a very strange feeling every time I talked to him.
However, it was a good feeling, I think, and eventually I couldn't stop talking to him nor thinking about him; he became a very important part of my day.
I thought, what if he was the missing part that I was searching for and needed the most?
But, wait, am I in love?

Chapter 2

E rik's words never stopped impressing me and the way he talked, oh, that made me really melt every time we talked. I just knew he was different but in what way, I couldn't say at that time as I was absolutely in love with him. I couldn't see his defects at all.

But for Erik, it was a bit different, saying lovely words that melts you, and replies was just what he did with others like me.
Being a gentleman or, in other words, being fake.
While on the other hand, I, Cassandra Daryl, was absolutely in love with him. Day by day, I was falling even harder.
He made me fly, shine, and glow with happiness. I really didn't know if he had feelings for me or not, but sooner or later, I was going to confess my love for him. I woke up the next day happy as usual, waiting to text him and start my day. Then I found this message from him:

"Cassandra, I really can't keep it a secret anymore but I LOVE YOU."
At this moment, I couldn't believe my eyes; I thought that I was still dreaming, my heart didn't stop beating as I started feeling the beats and hearing the sound of my breath that I couldn't control nor hold. But it was real, he had just confessed his love.
"I love you too, so much," I happily and blindly replied.
Our love story just started and I was the happiest, most-fortunate girl ever because the man that I loved and admired had just confessed his love and I no longer had to hide my feelings anymore. Now I could love him, have him forever, and I could call him MINE.

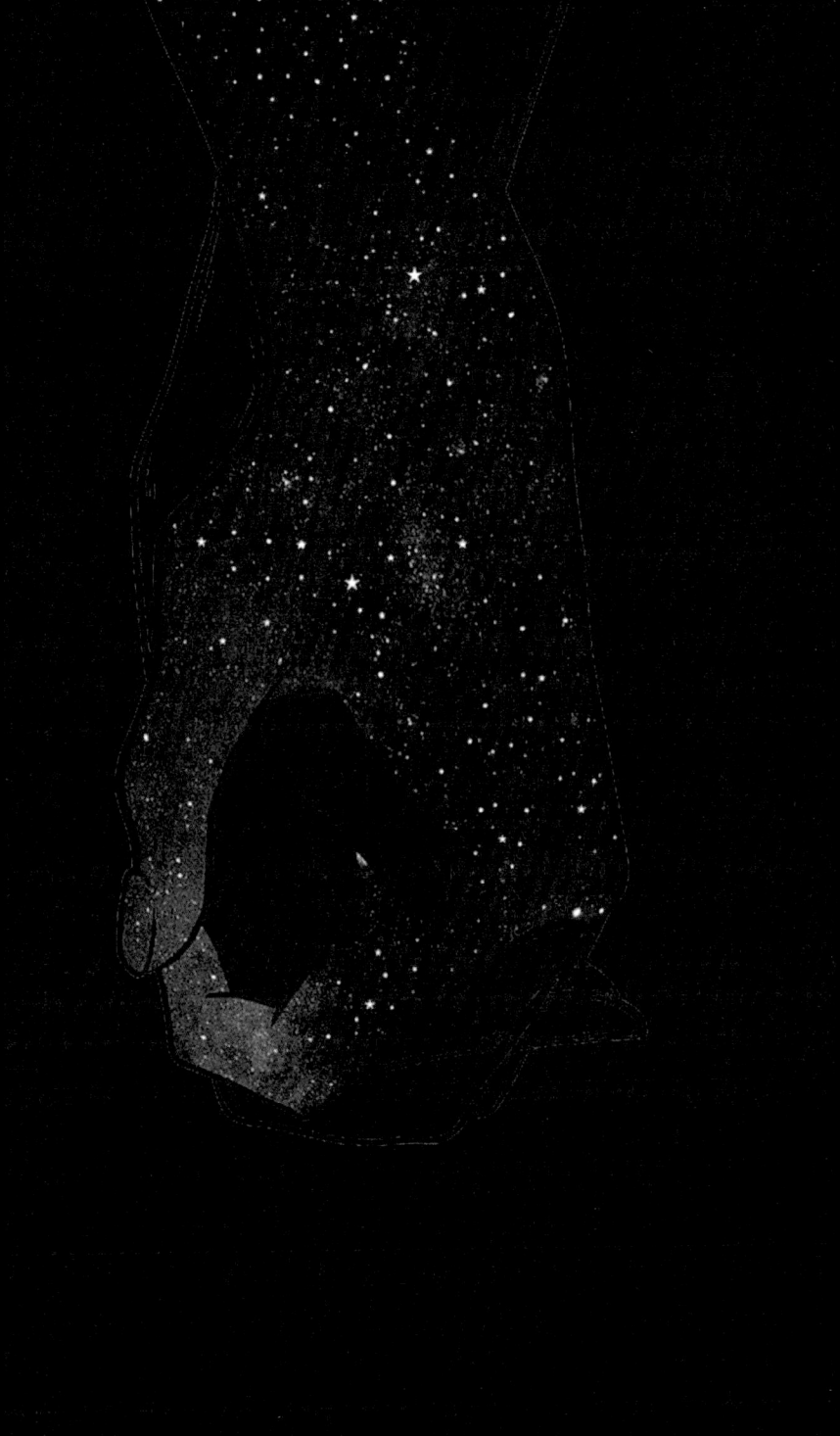

At this moment, I forgot all about my mind and my heart as he had stolen both of them. My mind that couldn't think about anything but Erik and my heart that was only beating his love. I lost sense of life and I started living in his world.
But was I even myself anymore?
I couldn't answer that question at that time, I didn't even recognize the change that I was going through.
All I felt at that period of time was only happiness.

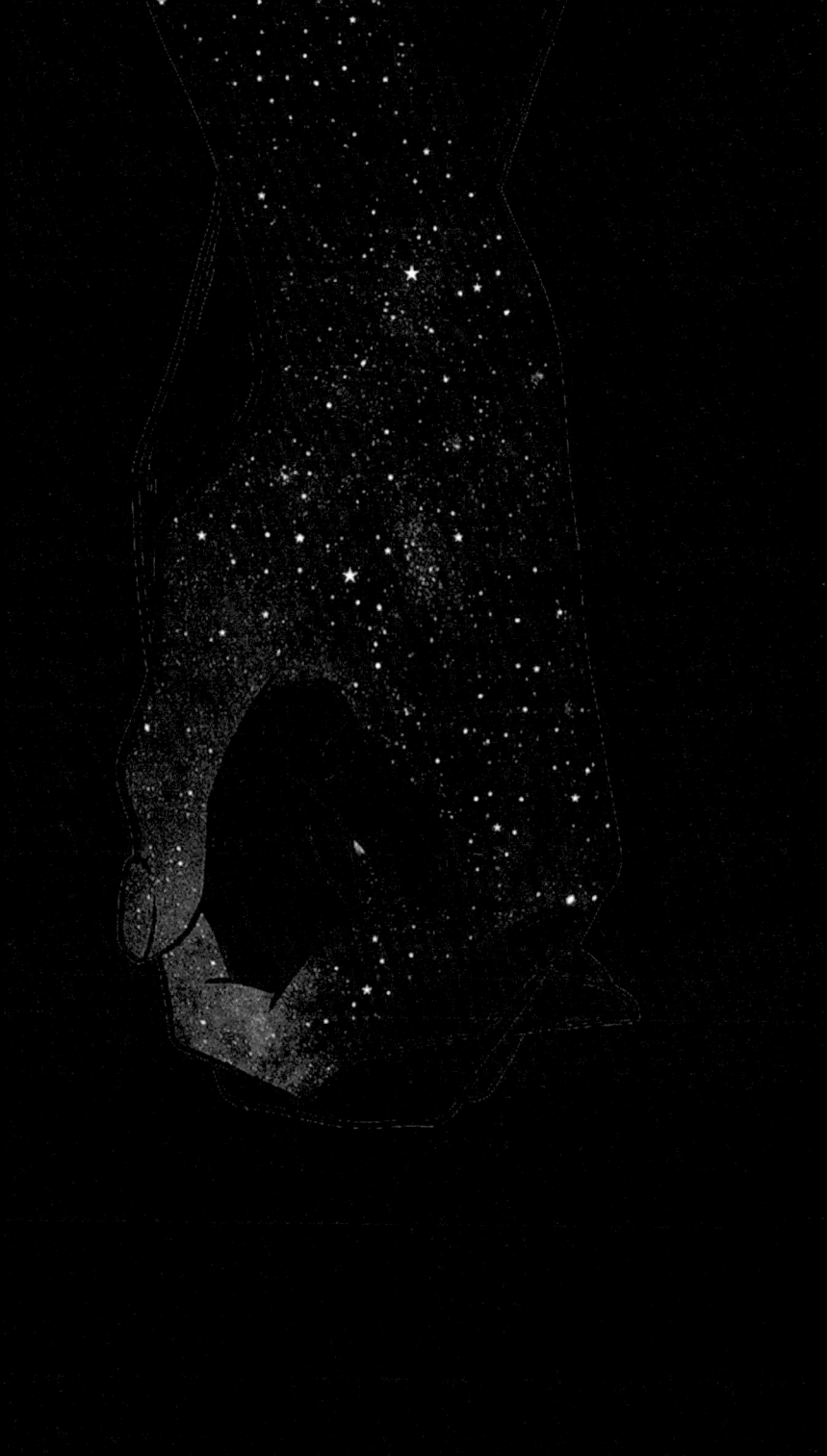

Chapter 3

A new bright morning started, it was a memorable day for me as it was the first morning with my love, Erik. Texting him with love. I woke up every day just to talk to him. I escaped from the outside world with him, he was my only shelter.

I was smiling the entire day while reading his words
and hearing his voice. He made me feel safe
and wanted.
I felt his presence even though he was not there. He
was living in my soul, heart, and mind. He was not only
a part of me but also inside me. A part can be taken
from you but I loved him so much that no one could
ever take him or touch him. I made my heart his only
home so now he was untouchable.
Erik lived there, but I was not sure if I lived in his heart
too or not. But how could I even know?
Few days later, I received a call from my dad saying
that Mom is sick and her situation is really urgent and
that he has to fly her to a European country for her
treatment. I was really shocked; I couldn't think nor
do anything.

I was far away from my parents and I couldn't go see my mom as Dad had said I wouldn't help in anything if I showed up there and that I should stay and continue my studies, but I was really worried about my mom. However, all I had to do was to pray for her every day, she is my everything. I literally can't do anything without her. So at this period of time, I was really passing through a very tough time and I couldn't focus on my studies. I was calling Dad few times a day to check up on my mom. And thank God, she was getting better every day.

I told Erik everything and he really stood by my side, as he always did, and warmed me with his love and words. He was so gentle, charming, and a good listener that I forgot my sadness.

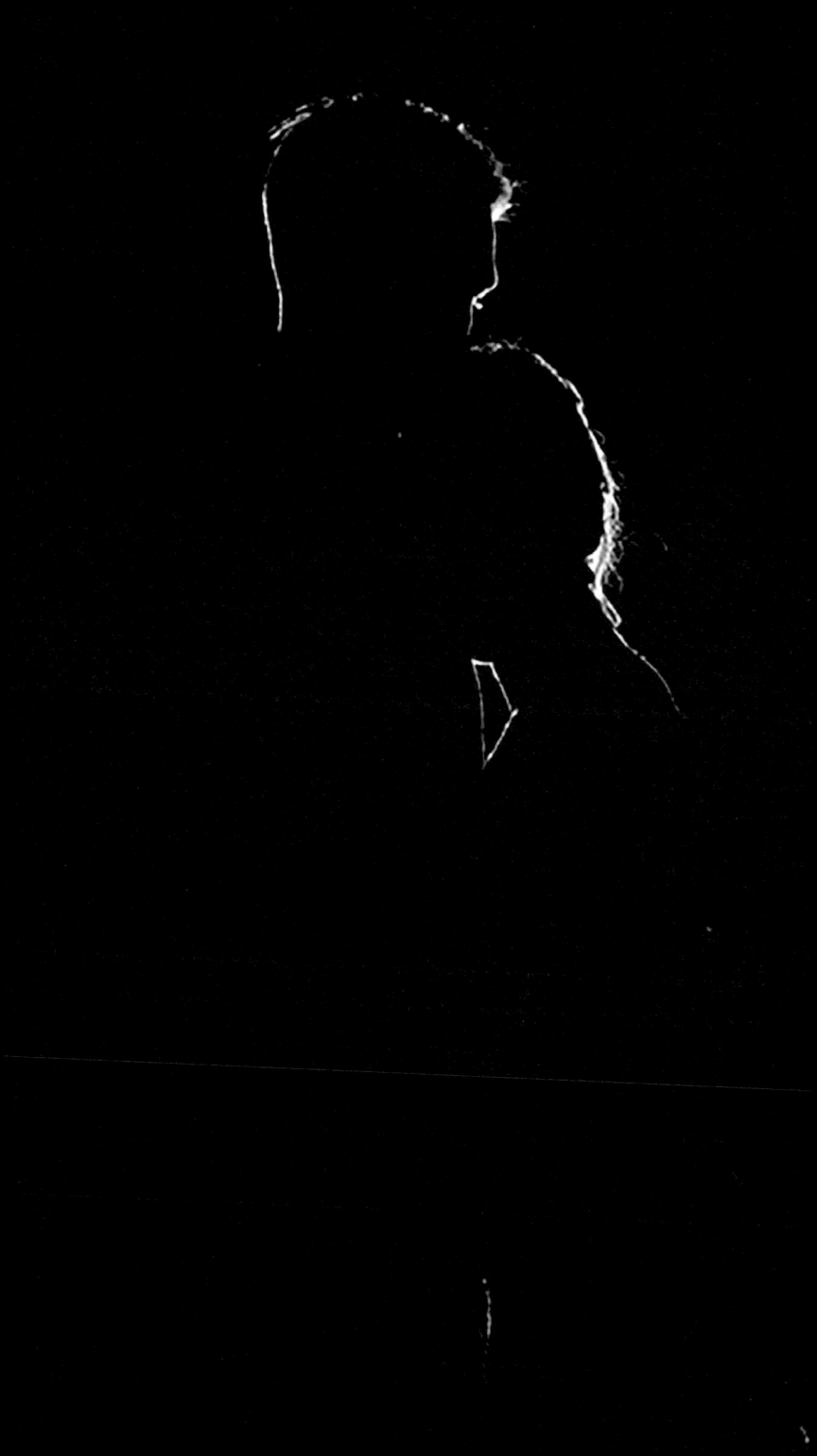

"I am always here for you and I will make you forget your pain once I see you, love. I will cure your body with a very warm hug of mine, I will wipe up your tears and kiss your forehead princess," he said softly.
I imagined him saying these words in front of me, and I, in a scene of love, watch his lips moving with an absolute admiration.
Those words just melted my heart that I couldn't reply but I saved those words in my heart and soul. Actually, his words gave me life.
And there was a very famous sentence that he always used to tell me and I can still remember it now; I can't forget it and I still can hear it coming out of his mouth.
"YOU ARE MINE!" he once said.

That sentence made feel safe and owned by only one man. I couldn't even look at any other man. Because Erik was all I could see.
I believed I no longer had to worry about losing him. We were stuck together till the end now.
I was deeply in love with him, so much that I believed each and every word he said and I followed his words and orders blindly.
"Yes, love. Sure, love, anytime you want," I replied to whatever he asked. In fact, I didn't know how to say "No" to him. However, there was something that I didn't notice at this period of time. Erik was taking advantage of my love and asked me to do everything for him. But how could I even know that the love of my life was playing me as if I was his doll. I was being deceived by my Erik.
How painful!

Days passed and we met. For me, that day was like a dream come true. I prepared myself as if it was my wedding day and not just a normal date. I wore new clothes; a black pants and a very elegant maroon blouse with my black, soft hair flying in the air, just as happy as I was that day. Erik was there in the restaurant, the restaurant that I chose, waiting for me. He was smiling so hard that I could see his white teeth and adoring lips looking at me. He was really handsome, with soft brown skin, brown eyes, tall, elegant, and he wore black pants just like me and a white t-shirt.
What a coincidence! I thought.
Erik was just what I wanted, and in my eyes, he was the most handsome man ever, even if he was not that handsome in other's eyes. But who would even care, what's important was that my eyes couldn't see anyone but him, only Erik.

I sat down in front of him, I couldn't say a word. Meanwhile, he reached his hands to hold mine and kissed my hands as he said, "Hi, love, you look gorgeous."

At this moment, I was literally melting and with each and every second passing, I was falling in love even harder. We talked and talked. It was the perfect day and then he brought me home and left. I was really happy and I started thinking about what we had done the whole day.

I just wished I had a power, the power of time. I wished I could stop that day and create a loop, a loop that would make this day happen again and again and again forever. It would be the perfect loop. And I didn't mind living the same day over and over again

I couldn't stop thinking about him and seeing him every day with the same events was all I wanted. Seconds with him, minutes, hours, days, weeks, months, year, a life with him. With my Erik!
What else could I need except a world where Erik and I were together?!

But there was something that I couldn't stop thinking about but I didn't know whether to believe it or not. It was quite strange.
When we met, I looked so deep into his eyes and the way he looked at me didn't make me feel secure; instead, I felt scared and I immediately felt that this man was going to leave me one day. I really didn't know how I felt

this but his looks were just saying the opposite of what his mouth was saying.
His mouth said, "I will never leave you" and his eyes said, I will leave you.
But I didn't know which one to believe. But at the end, I loved him so much and trusted him so I ignored the looks in his eyes.

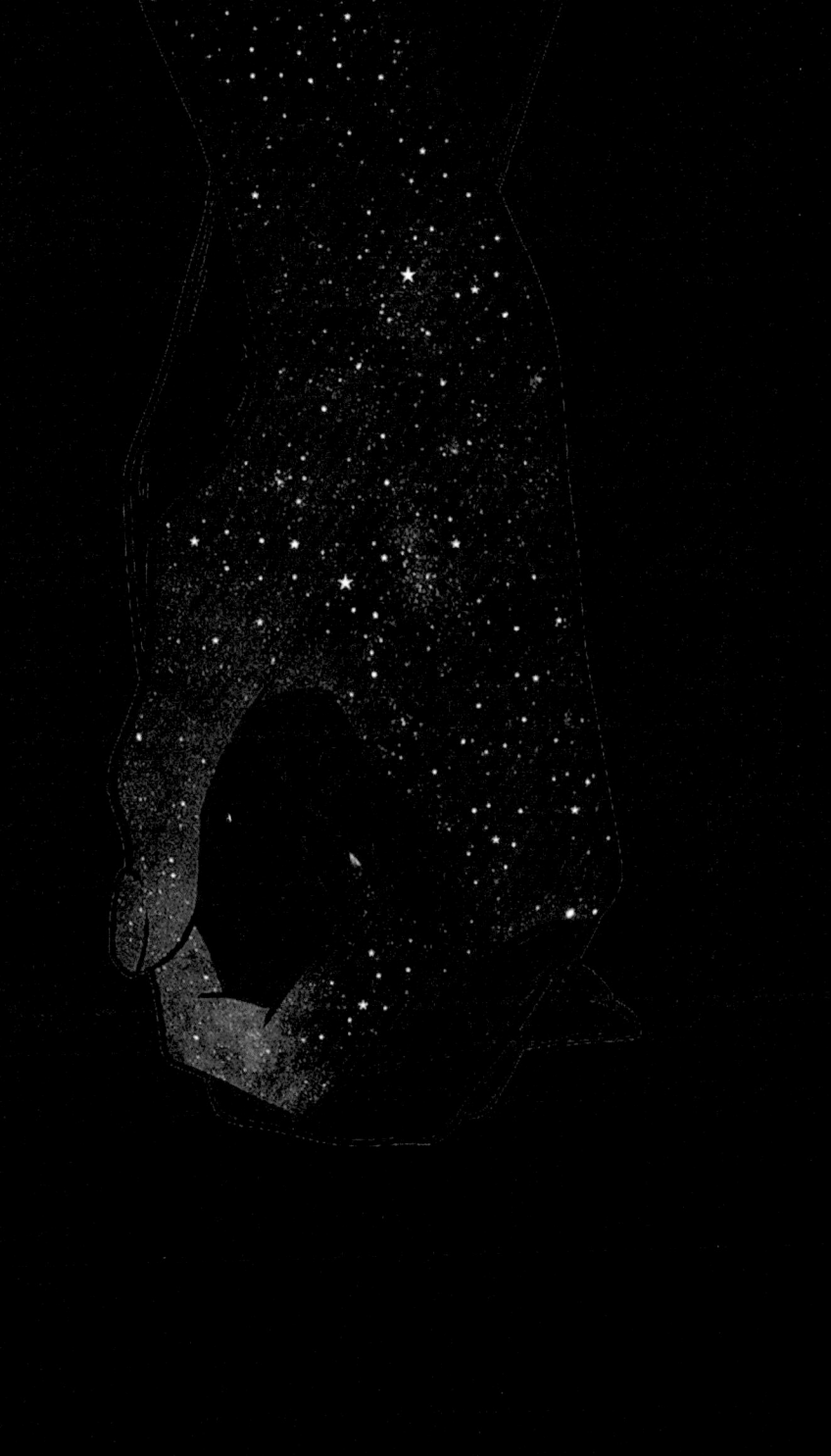

Chapter 4

Days passed and we talked a lot and met several times. But day after day, Erik was changing. He started answering late and stopped calling me every day as he used to do. I was really missing him. And I didn't know what was going on.

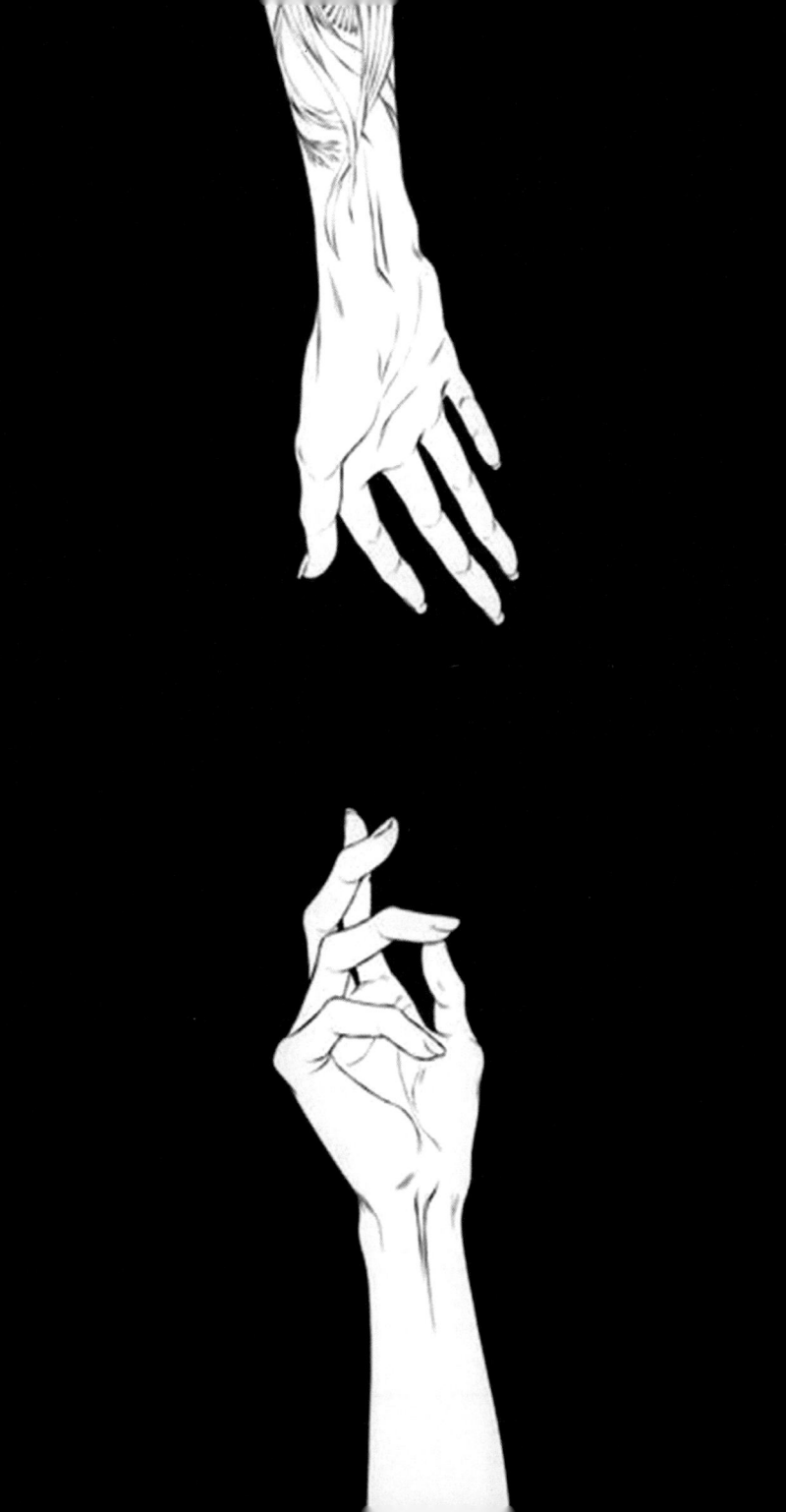

But then, he started fighting over silly stuff and fighting for no reason sometimes.
Have I done anything wrong? I started wondering. Or maybe he is just busy and doesn't have time to call.
But anyway, I trusted him and loved him so I kept finding excuses for him and forgiving him every time. And I waited and waited for him every day to finish his work so that we could talk, I knew he was stressed so I didn't ask him why he had changed so much with me. But my love for him never changed; I treated him with love every single day, even though he didn't do the same. I kept him so comfortable and did everything he asked me to do and more but still he was going away and left me.

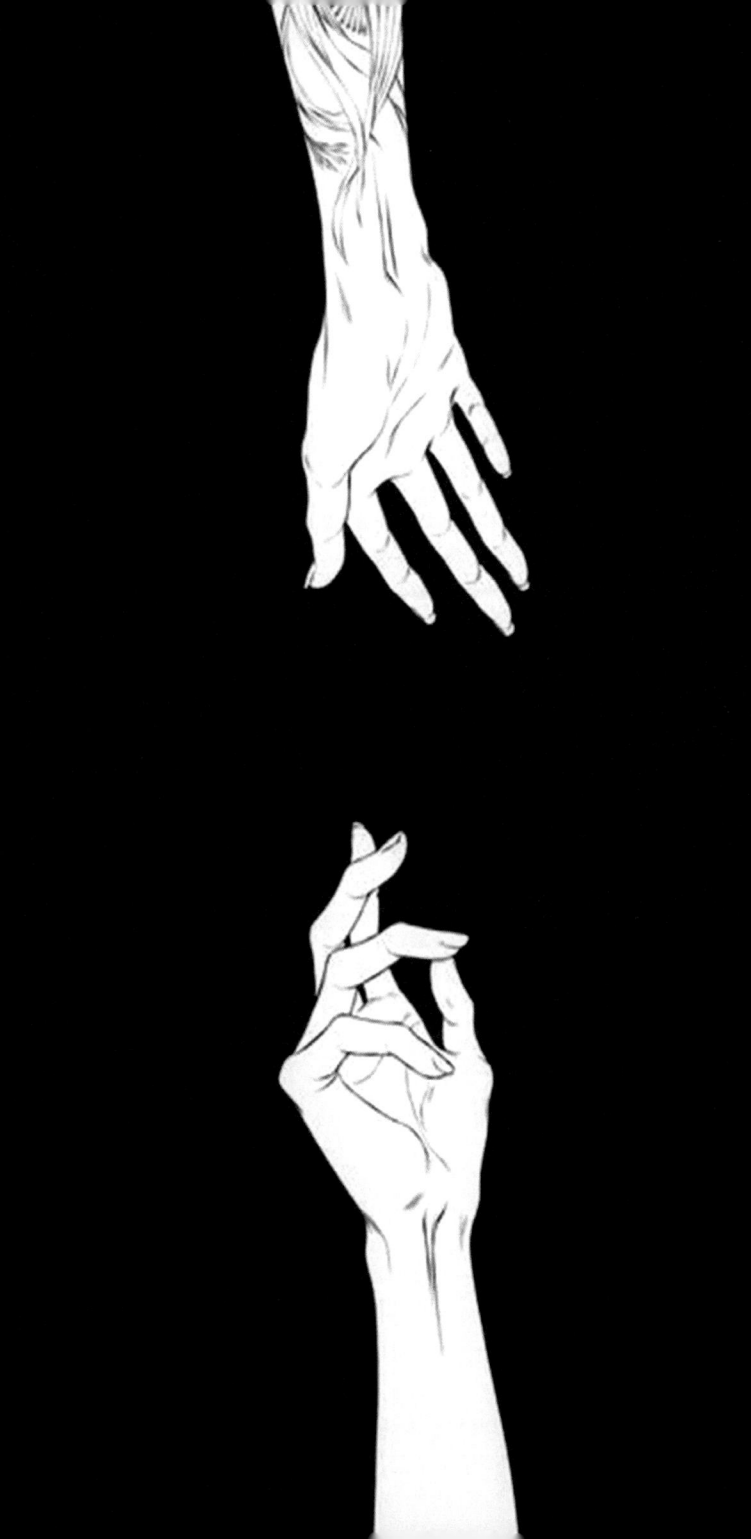

Every time we fought, I was always the one who was saying "sorry" even if it was his mistake. I told myself it was OK, just apologize, it's just one word, and I didn't want to lose him. Only one word would get us back together but I didn't know that that one word was not working. In fact, Erik didn't want me anymore. It was over for him.

So here it came; one day, he fought a very big fight with me because I disobeyed him in something he asked me to do. He really talked to me in such a very bad and offensive way that I was completely shocked. This was not our first fight but he had never talked to me that way nor offended me that way.

"Cassandra, have you lost your mind? I am Erik, no one can say no to me nor disobey me," my Erik said with anger and hatred in his voice, a tone of voice that I had never heard before from my love.

I was like, *What? Who is that guy?* That's not my Erik.
"Erik, what's going on? Why all that rage? It's not a big deal," I replied softly.
"Look, I don't want to talk about it anymore. I will sleep now. Bye," he said at last.
And that was the last message I received from him. It's like he had been looking for any excuse to leave me or rather abandon me. In fact, at that moment I didn't know that these words would be his last to me. I had thought that he would text me the next day to say sorry or to give me an excuse for what he said. However, it was his goodbye message.

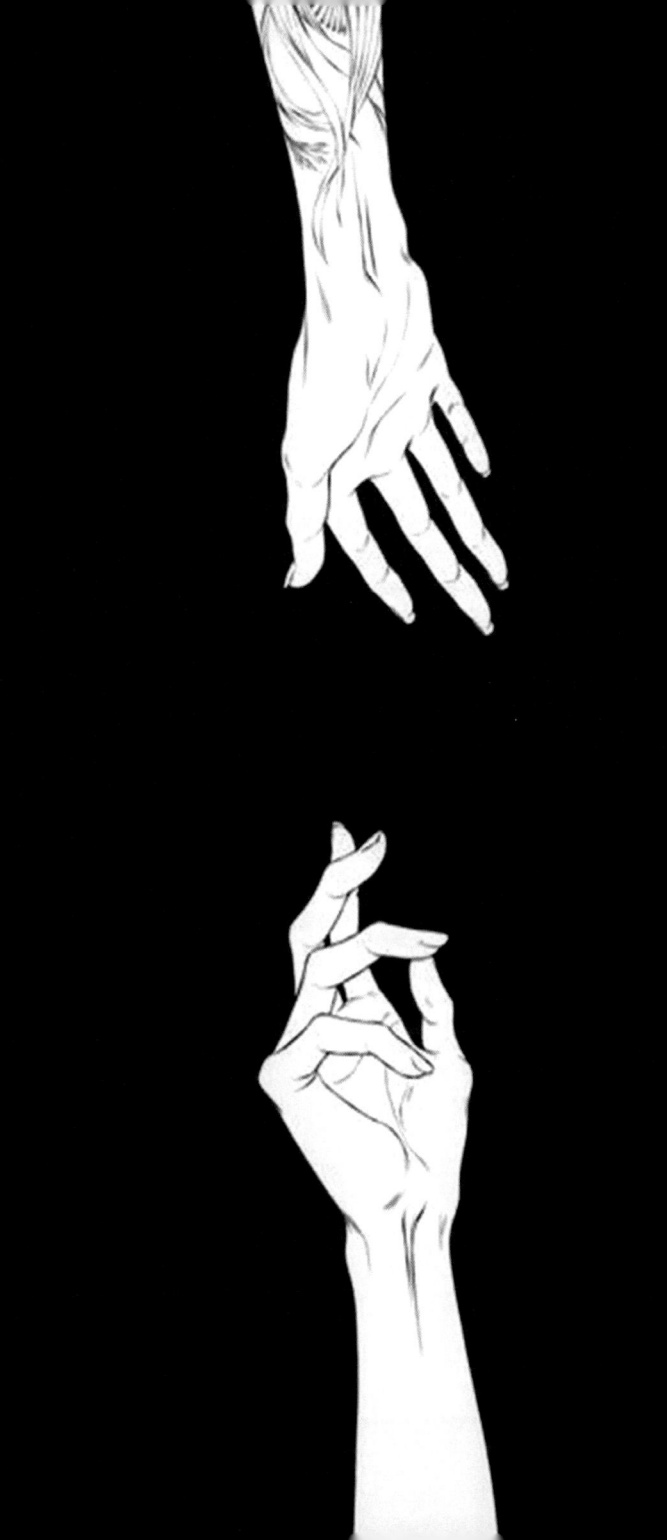

I couldn't text him because what he said that day
stopped me from texting him. I waited hours, days,
weeks, and months.
What a long time, isn't it?
But the truth is that I couldn't believe he abandoned
me I thought our love was strong enough and deep
enough that we would not be able to live without
each other. They say that love is strong or was it me
who loved him so hard? Or was it my mistake from the
beginning that I fell in love?

I asked you, "Will you stay?"
"Forever," you had said.

Four months passed and I was still waiting. I still couldn't believe that it was all a lie, that I was living in a sea of lies, that his love was a lie. In fact, he had never loved me but it was me who loved him.

But why did you even lie? Why did you take me to your fantasy, inexistent world of love? What have I done to you? Is it because I loved you so hard? What about trusting you and giving you my heart? I did everything to make you happy. I was ready to love you forever. I was ready to give you everything.
But maybe everything was not enough or maybe everything was just too much for you.
You deserved much less than everything. You simply didn't deserve me. I was too much for you, too valuable for you to hold.

And what was the world for me except my Erik?

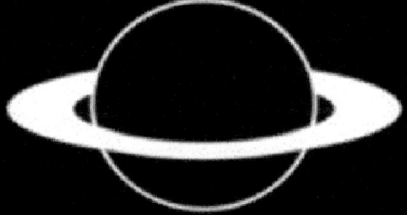

That night, everything changed and since then my life has become worse, I cried and cried. I cried every night. I cried so hard that my eyes were red the whole day and my eyes ran out of tears. Everything was falling apart as if the whole world was against me, as if the whole world had let me down, and what was the world for me except my Erik? And as he failed me, now the world was nothing but a nightmare that I couldn't avoid.

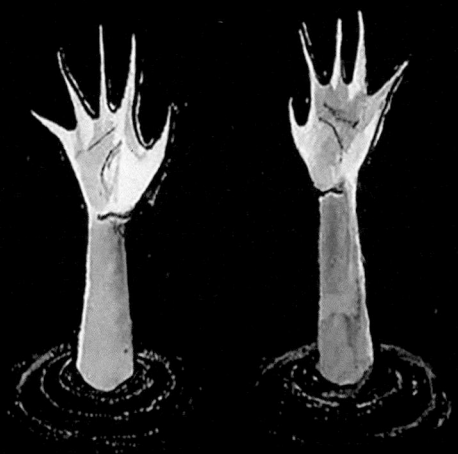

Chapter 5

Living in this nightmare felt so hard. It was hard for me to stop thinking about him or forget him. I needed him to help me go through this nightmare but how could he help me when he was the one who left me there!
They say memories are painful and for me that was quite real.

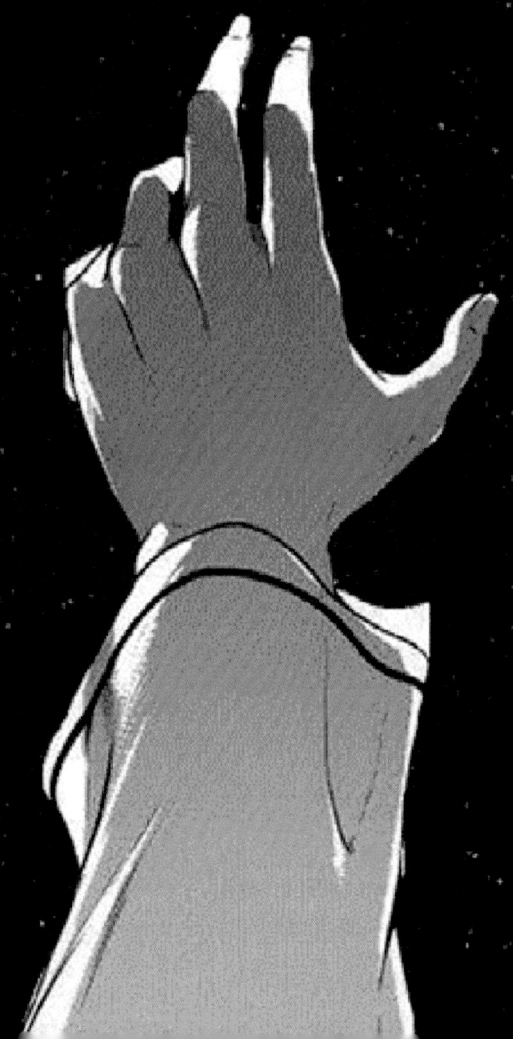

How can I forget his words that made me feel safe and wanted? How can I forget the nights we used to spend together? How can I forget his kiss on my hands that day?

How can I forget my first love? I started wondering as I remembered that day when I met him. I was really sad, angry, and crying, because I had some issues with my relatives. But then I saw him and I ran so fast, heading toward my Erik, and hugged him so tight that I stopped crying.

"It's OK, I am here now," he had whispered in my ears. So how am I supposed to forget all that?

I just wanted him to be the first and the last, to be the owner of my heart and the hunter of my soul. Sometimes, I feel lost without him, I feel like I want to have him back. He was all I wished for.

And darkness started consuming my soul and my thoughts.

I tried to end my life several times but I failed every time I tried. I couldn't bear that pain. It made me half dead. My desire and love for life was gone. Life wasn't anything but a pain, a very huge pain that I wished for death every day.

My mind couldn't stop thinking about what he did and what a fool he me made look like. The way he treated me and the way he left so easily. Believing all that was hard enough to make me want to end my life and set my soul free once and for all. I tried and tried to kill myself but every time, God would delay my death time, as if He was giving me another chance to live. I didn't know why He did that. I didn't have a purpose in life anymore so why did He still want me to live? I was dead already.

I reached a point that made me feel that he was not the right guy. He was fake and I was real. So how could we be together again? We didn't fit together, we didn't belong to each other, and we were never meant to be together. That was a fact and I had to accept it.
Maybe I gave my love to the wrong guy but I was still thankful for him because this experience made me discover myself and let me see that I should never trust anyone but myself. Because I won't let myself down but people will always do.
They say time heals but it depends on how much time do you need to heal, and for me, years were not even enough. And whenever I remember him, it all comes to my mind as if it all happened yesterday.

I was still living in his own world with all his memories. Unable to escape.

I can still remember each and every single detail as if it is all engraved in my head. I can still remember his beautiful smell; one day, I bought the same perfume he used, so that every time I used it, I could feel him beside me, I could feel his presence.

Also I can still remember his work schedule, his breaks, and his leaving time. I was still living my days according to his. I kept checking his profile every day to see how he was doing, was he fine? I was checking his posts too, to see if he was posting anything about me or maybe he missed me.

But, in fact, I didn't find what I was wishing for. However, he was traveling from here to there, posting funny stuff, and it was as if we hadn't broken up

His memories kept on killing me every day, and for him, he just forgot everything the night he left me. So it seemed like I had to do the same and let it go.
But again, my poisoned memories that he left behind kept on spreading all over my soul, until it left me half dead.
A body without a heart, a body without a soul that admires life and wanted to live and shine. A dreaming soul and a very innocent girl was being destroyed by her only love and the only one she trusted. I gave him my heart without even thinking and without regretting it even once. Because I once thought he was mine.

Will this broken heart ever be fixed?

I became the new Erik...

I was an innocent, pure angel and not capable of doing harm to anyone. I thought I was living with angels like me, pure people but, in fact, they were devils hidden behind faces of angels. Devils that fooled angels like me, manipulated them with their angelic acts of honor, and made them one of them. They enjoyed playing us like dolls, until we became newborn devils. Darkness became our only refuge. And hurting people became our only job and enjoyment.

So I started hurting people just like what Erik did to me. I started hurting their feelings with words like poison and acts of demons that tore them apart yet they were still alive but with no life inside of them. I didn't really care about their feelings nor who they were because for me, they were all devils just like Erik; killing us and acting as if they did nothing.

I became the NEW Erik.

I lost myself. Lost who I once was. I fought myself but still couldn't change who I had become. I saw his eyes in everybody's. I took revenge from the people I knew as if they were him. I didn't recognize that I was making a mistake, losing the people who loved me and cared about me. But, unfortunately, I couldn't see anyone but Erik. He changed me to someone I couldn't recognize nor control anymore.

With time, I started remembering who I once used to be. And started convincing myself that he didn't deserve this innocent, lovely girl and her heart that was full of love for him. And yes, he was my only hero, I imagined him in every heroic situation in movies.

"I've got my hero now." I used to say this sentence every time I watched a movie. But eventually, I realized heroes will always stay in movies and books. I think they were written to stay there, in our imaginations

Chapter 6

Few years passed. Now I was adapted to life without him. I knew he wouldn't text me again. I convinced myself that he had left. So I started living my life even though I was not able to forget him because he was my first love, he formed a part of me, he lived in my heart and in my soul and I

I let him go, just like the smoke in the air. He's gone and can never come back.

can't just delete him from my history because my heart won't allow it.
On the other hand, I started getting myself busy. I started focusing more on my studies. I had been wasting time with him; I left it all behind for him and dedicated my time only to him, but now it was my time. I almost forgot that I am a writer. I used to write stories, songs, and poems as well.
So this time, I decided to heal myself through getting myself busy improving my talent. I decided to recover myself by myself. So I wrote my first poem, and named it *Drugged love.*
It's my favorite poem because it describes how hard this experience was for me and how hard it is to live in a world of lies, that makes you feel really happy and in one second, it can make you feel sad, that makes

you feel worth it and the next day you are nothing, that makes you feel strong but, in fact, it's making you weaker with time, that makes you feel loved but, in fact, you are being used, you are being manipulated by the only one you trusted and loved. Welcome to the fake world that you once thought was real.

Drugged Love

Your love was like a drug.
You drugged me and brought me into your world.
You made me unconscious.

I loved it there, I thought your world was my home but I didn't know it was fake.

Until I woke up, I opened my eyes and it was all dark and you were not there.
Where are you? Am I lost? I wondered.
In fact, it took me time realizing that you had just left me there.

You drugged me and left me on my own. But I can only remember the good things that happened between us.
It will always be our little secret.
I still have your words buried down in my soul and my heart still carries you, even though I tried to let you go. But I couldn't, so I think you are stuck with me forever, in my memory.

But what a strong drug!

Well, that poem won the best poem in the writing competition in the university. It was one of my biggest achievements. I turned my bad, failed, and negative experience into a successful one. I turned the game now. Now I lead my life.

I started reciting my poems at international events and events in the university. People loved hearing me, hearing the struggle they were once afraid to talk about, taking the courage from my words to move on from toxic relationships, love relationships, friendships, or even family relationships.

Relationships are not permanent. You have to put that in mind so that you can easily let go. And you have to know that anyone can leave no matter how many years or how much time have you guys spent together

Say goodbye and start a new life.

Time; days, weeks, months, and years will disappear once that person doesn't need you anymore. People come into your life to stay for a little while and then leave, but some stay. Those who leave will definitely leave you a lesson to learn and a new strong piece will build within you.
I always say if you find yourself in a relationship where the other side doesn't appreciate your presence, doesn't treat you the way you deserve, doesn't love you enough, doesn't care about your feelings, always hurts you, and never apologizes, then just leave. Sometimes saying "goodbye" is better than saying "come back."
I can't even count how many times did I say "goodbye."

You will light up again even though it's too dark.

Treat these kind of people with total ignorance and accept the fact that you are not wanted by this person because once you accept that, you will move on so easily. Because there are people out there waiting to get only your attention. So wait, observe, learn, and choose. Because now you are qualified to choose the right person.

Chapter 7

At one of the events I attended, he was there. I didn't really know why he was there nor who invited him, but I didn't really care. I can't deny that I was surprised and my heart started beating fast when I saw him. However, one side of me was saying, "I miss him," and the other side was saying, "Just ignore him like he did."

So I did it and ignored him but he couldn't ignore me. He couldn't take his eyes off me. He was surprised as well when he saw me and he heard my poems as well, as I was one of the participants that night.

I finished and sat with my friends when he came by.

"Hi, Cassandra. How are you?" he said with his eyes glowing, the eyes I once used to admire. He seemed happy to see me again.

"Fine. What about you?" I replied with confidence and careless attitude, and it was as if I didn't care who he was anymore.

I felt nothing talking to him, it's like his effect over me was gone. I didn't care what he was saying neither what he was doing.

But he was looking at me with an absolute admiration because now he was looking at the new version of me. The most beautiful and successful one.
I didn't care about that look either, I felt like it was too late to give me that look.
Where was that look when we were together? Where was all that respect? But you can't turn back time.
Now remembering him doesn't hurt me anymore.
Time healed me but time can never make me forget.
But time can teach you how to accept and acceptance is the key of recovery and success. Just like what it did to me.
So I accepted the fact that we were not meant to be together. And I love myself so much that I didn't need him anymore, his presence is no longer desired

He is out now and I am in. I lead the game now and Erik was a player who lost the game, but I won and I will keep on wining because I am the leader and this is my life.

Chapter 8

Here I am standing by myself. As I see no one who deserves to stand by me. I have friends beside me yet I don't need the help of anyone. I passed through all this pain alone. Nobody could ever feel how desperate, shocked, and hurt I felt, and I wasn't able to describe that pain.

I was bleeding yet I didn't find someone to stop the pain. So why will I need anyone now?
I now know my value, my worth, and what I am capable of. So the presence of people and love is no longer desired and is no longer what I am looking for because now I am looking for myself. Treating it well, understanding it, healing it, and loving it.
Just put this in mind, no one will ever feel you except you. People will hear you for two reasons; one, they will listen and do nothing, they listen to either laugh and make fun of your story and underestimate your pain. And two, they will go out there and tell people how desperate you are.
They simply won't understand your pain and suffering as much as you do. So either way, they won't help you. However, if they did understand you, they won't help as well

because at this specific time, you will only need yourself, yourself, and yourself.
Many people may see that being alone is a bad thing or it means that you are unsociable. But, in fact, you are not. You are just healing, understanding yourself, recovering from what they did.
They will only hurt you but they can never heal you because those who hurt you can never be the ones to heal you. They will do nothing but keep on hurting you over and over again, and keep on letting you down.
Some people enter your life to either light you up or turn you off. But both ways, you will learn because you will know who deserves you and who doesn't. You may really get hurt by some of them but trust me, this will make you nothing but stronger and more mature.
Don't let this take you down, just rise up again and move on and

you will move on; trust me, I have been there before. Grave pain, tears all over your face, and having that feeling that the whole world let you down and there is no one by your side. Darkness will conquer your soul, heart, and your whole life. But don't let it win. Go inside there and light yourself up with taking care of it, discovering it, and changing it to nothing but the best. Appreciate each and every moment you are spending with yourself. It's worth your time.

Live your life and keep knowing more people, keep learning, and keep changing. Spread love and make friends but don't get too close, you might get hurt. As I always do, I expect anything from anyone, nobody is perfect and neither am I.

Value yourself and only yourself.

On the other hand, don't fall in love again, don't fall in love again unless you find someone who treats you better than you treat yourself, who loves you for who you are, and not for what you have, who appreciates your presence and values your worth. YOU ARE A TREASURE.

Message to Erik:
Thanks for making me who I am now. Your absence helped create my presence. Your absence made me discover myself and made me recognize that I don't belong to anyone but myself.
I own no one and no one owns me. I own myself.

The End